The Shepherd's Crook

~From the Star to the Cross~

A Novelette

By

JOE SHUMOCK

Printed in the United States of America

Copyright: Joe Shumock 2019
Publisher: Silver Sage Media
www.SilverSageMedia.com
Contact: Info@SilverSageMedia.com

Paperback ISBN: 978-0-9897201-8-2
Ebook ISBN: 978-0-9897201-9-9

Jacket Design and Author Photo: Barry Hodgin

Interior Design: Darlene Swanson, www.Van-Garde.com

Developmental Editing, Copyediting, Writer's Coaching:
Wayne South Smith, www.waynesouthsmith.com

To my mother, Leona Shumock
(1903 - 1995) She would have
loved this story.

And to my dad, Frank Shumock
(1902 - 1953) Gone from my
life much too soon.

And, as always,
for Kathy

Books by Joe Shumock

The Letter Series:
A Letter to Die For
The Lost Letter
Letter From the Dark
Sacrifice of the Lambs

For Young Audiences:
Briana and the Dog

About the Author:

JOE SHUMOCK WAS BORN AND raised in Semmes, near Mobile, Alabama. After serving 3 1/2 years in the U.S. Army, Shumock earned a Batchelor of Science degree in accounting from the University of New Orleans. His career as a CPA and Certified Financial Planner lasted until he retired in 2002.

Joe currently lives in Foley, Alabama.

The author has been writing and publishing since 2007. The Shepherd's Crook is Shumock's sixth story. It is his second undertaking outside the Letter Series, a continuing collection of mystery/suspense thrillers.

Shumock is currently working on three new stories including a fifth novel in the Letter Series, the second in the Briana trilogy and the first in another family trilogy of a grandfather forced by circumstance to raise his two young granddaughters.

~ *From the Star* ~

As the sun faded beyond the horizon, the boy turned and looked eastward for the star that had appeared a fortnight ago. It was there again, rising now between the hills. Unlike other stars, this one seemed so near. The boy's father and uncles watched too, talking in hushed tones about its meaning. Shepherds were familiar with the night sky and realized this star should not be there.

The boy—his name was Alon—had recently turned thirteen years of age. His slim boyish body was starting to fill out; muscles were becoming defined and he was growing taller. He would soon be caring for a herd of his own, and often, he dreamed of those times.

Tonight though, with the soft sound of bleating sheep in the background, Alon listened to conversations among his elders. His own family and other shepherds from nearby valleys had gathered. Some were excited while others were worried. The shepherds did not like changes in their world, and several were afraid. All of them were fascinated and concerned about the strange star.

The men were nomadic shepherds, spending many days distant from their homes. Any reason to gather and talk was welcomed. An uncle wondered aloud, "Perhaps our location in these hills causes the star to appear different and strange."

Another questioned, "Maybe it has been there all along and we did not notice?"

An argument ensued, everyone quickly taking sides.

"I study the sky each night," someone said. "The star is new. I am sure of it."

"We notice the brightness of the star because we are standing high on these hills," another stated. He waved an arm toward the valley below. "I did not see it when I was with my herd."

"The star was hiding behind the hills when you were in the valley, old fool," a friend teased as he poked the man with a finger.

Alon's father spoke up. "I don't think our location matters."

The others quieted, turning to listen.

Continuing, the boy's father said almost in a whisper, "I believe we are witnessing something out of the ordinary ..." His words trailed off as the shepherds all looked toward the star.

Alon believed his father.

The two of them had noticed the star several nights earlier, not long after it first appeared. They had been walking near their herd looking for signs of the wolves that had recently taken two young ewes. Alon had been the first to draw attention to the star, noting its glow as they walked in the valley.

"Why is that star so bright?" Alon had asked.

When he pointed it out to his father, the older man stopped. He had gazed at this particular star and then at others in the eastern sky. Alon watched and could tell his father was interested and even surprised at what he saw. He kept looking back and forth between this new star and others nearby.

Softly, almost to himself, Alon's father murmured, "It isn't moving in the sky like the other stars." After a few moments, he turned to Alon and added, "I have never witnessed that before."

The two of them had watched, waiting for it to disappear or

change. It had remained the same that evening and each evening since, appearing at dusk and seeming to hover low over the hills at the same place in the sky each night.

Tonight, Alon's uncles and other shepherds stood near the road at a large rocky outcropping. They were at the upper rim of the small valley where most of their flocks were grazing. All of them were looking at the sky, some in groups while others stood alone.

Glancing often at the star, the shepherds spoke with lowered voices, some almost reverent.

"Could it be a miracle," an old shepherd questioned, "… a sign from heaven?"

Glancing at the old man, another said, "There are prophesies foretold in ancient writings. Perhaps we are witnessing one of these."

Others thought since the evening was clear, the star might be more visible than usual. A few continued arguing that because of their location, they might just have a better view.

As some argued about the star itself, Alon's father and a few of the older men spoke in hushed tones of prophecies they had heard since childhood.

"A Messiah will come to be our King," one said. "I have always been told this."

The men glanced at each other. It was easy to hope for such a leader.

The Jewish people had been treated poorly by the Romans for as long as most could remember. Everyone there could tell of an experience. Alon's father looked to the hills, his eyes glistening. Late in life, his own father had been run down and crippled by a Roman soldier on horseback.

For generations, they had held out hope for a savior to come and free them from their oppression. Could this finally be the time?

The sun had disappeared completely now, and the shepherds continued to watch the star as the night grew darker. Other tradesmen and travelers along the dusty road had stopped and joined the discussions. They kept a watchful eye. Mounted Roman soldiers often passed along this road, and Jews in groups of any sort were frequently challenged.

Many theories were being discussed there by the roadside. Alon listened quietly and tried to understand what was happening. Questions centered on where the star had come from, and what did it mean? Could this light be guiding shepherds and others to the Messiah?

"I do not know what to think of it," Alon's father said as he scratched at his beard. It was obvious he was as confused as all the others.

At last, weary of the arguments, Alon tugged at his father's robe, pulling him aside. "Father," the boy implored, "allow me to go and see if there is a truth to what the elders remember of the prophecies. Is there a Messiah at the place of the star? Could there really be someone who has come to lead us from our bondage and into a time of freedom and peace?"

Alon's father admired the depth of his son's questions. Looking at him, the father realized his son was approaching manhood though he was still young in years. Still, so much a part of his own heart, the old shepherd was understandably reluctant to allow his son to go beyond his protection. Could he permit Alon to follow this unusual star toward questions none here could answer nor understand?

Yet, considering all things, the father realized and understood in his own heart that he could not refuse Alon's request.

The boy stood quietly watching as his father worked toward a decision. He glanced at Alon occasionally while mumbling mostly to himself.

"I don't know where this journey will take you," the father said aloud. "And I have seen mounted Roman soldiers three times today." He looked at Alon. "What will you tell the soldiers if they stop you?"

"I will tell them I am searching for my father who is a shepherd," the boy said after a moment's thought. "I will say we are nomads and move about." Alon smiled then, thinking of something new. "I will say you are big and have a very black beard. I will ask if they have seen you." He smiled again. "I will ask questions until they are happy for me to be on my way."

The old shepherd laughed heartily and put an arm around his son's shoulder. He was satisfied the boy could handle himself. *Yes,* the father thought with a smile, *the Romans would probably be very happy to send my boy along his way.*

The decision was made. The father told Alon to prepare for a journey. Then he gathered food and other provisions for the boy. He also provided a skin of leather for Alon to wrap about his shoulders. The nights were cold in these hills. The leather would also keep his son dry and warm if rain came while he was on the road.

Standing near the evening fire, the boy shouldered his pack and prepared to leave. Finally, his father entrusted one last article to him. He handed Alon the shepherd's crook he had carried for as long as Alon could remember. The boy was surprised. The staff, on end, stood more than a head taller than Alon himself and almost as tall as his father.

The youngster recalled a story his father had told. As a small boy, Alon's father had watched his own father carve, mold, and then caringly oil and polish the staff. Its usefulness had been proven many times according to his father. There were stories of how wolves would attack, and the staff would be used to defend the sheep. Other stories told of using the crook to pull back lambs that had fallen beyond reach on some distant rocky hillside.

It was not only a tool of service but also one of beauty to be treasured and passed down from father to son in coming generations. This shepherd's crook was one of the most prized possessions in the family, and Alon's father was passing this treasure on to him.

"It is yours now," his father told him. Then, with a lowered voice, he added, "Your heart will tell you when it is time to pass this staff on to another shepherd."

Alon proudly carried the staff as he turned toward the road. Firelight allowed his father to watch as the boy glanced back and waved.

Alon's father stepped closer to the glowing coals and stood staring after his son. He could not imagine what he would do if some harm came to Alon. There was always the threat of losing the boy to the Romans, too. Still, Alon's father knew he had done everything he could to prepare his son for this uncertain venture.

The journey was long for the boy. Two nights and two days Alon walked, resting only when he became too tired to continue. He was watchful for the soldiers at all times and saw them on several occasions. Usually, he would hurry off the road and hide among the rocks and wildflowers until the men had passed. Once though, he was unable to get off the road. Boulders had left only a narrow pass, and there was no place to go and hide. Alon moved aside as much as possible and pressed himself against the rocks. The five soldiers were talking and laughing and only glanced his way as they rode along. Their horses came so close Alon could have reached out and touched them.

He slept under bushes when he rested at night using the leather skin his father had given him to keep warm. In the day-time, Alon napped in the shadow of rocks near the edge of the road. There were other travelers walking with him most of the time. Listening, he heard some of them speak of the star. They, too, wondered about its meaning.

The star was there as darkness fell each evening. The light was always where Alon expected, continuing to lead him to the east. Tired and hungry as evening approached on the second day, Alon came to the outskirts of a village. He heard others call it Bethlehem—in Judea. As he drew near the community, the boy realized he was nearing the end of his journey. The star he had been following appeared lower in the sky tonight, and closer. There was a warm glow about it now. Alon felt drawn to the star, allowing it to direct his final steps.

The tired and hungry boy looked ahead. Cobblestoned streets led to stone houses. In the distance, villagers could be seen enter-ing their homes. A few women and children were carrying the night's water home from the village well. Workmen could be seen putting away their tools. The day's activities were nearing an end.

As he entered the village, few people bothered to look his way. He was just a poor shepherd boy walking alone on Bethlehem's streets.

Alon peered ahead, seeing an inn. Just past it was a shed for animals. There, the star hovered, stationary.

The boy walked on to the stable. Alon felt heat from the animals even before he entered. The smell of fresh hay and the scent of the animals was heavy in the air. Glancing toward the inn where travelers were resting and taking nourishment, Alon could hear bits of conversation and sometimes even laughter. Those people were warm, their bellies full, and worries forgotten for the night.

As he entered the animal shed, Alon was drawn to a particular stall. A candle lantern hung from the rafters casting a glow on the scene before him. Everything was visible under the soft clear light.

A man and woman huddled at a manger where animals would normally eat. Alon crept closer, remembering the star and his journey and sensing he was seeing something exceptional. The star had led him to this.

Close finally, Alon realized there was a tiny baby on fresh straw in the manger. As he watched, the woman reached down to the little one, her hand cupping the baby's head and her fingers ever so gently caressing its cheeks. Though it was difficult to hear, Alon could tell the woman was humming softly to the child.

The baby was wrapped in swaddling clothes and rested quietly as the woman touched it with her finger tips. Alon realized the man and woman must be the baby's parents. Though others were watching from the shadows, these two were looking at the infant with obvious love and concern.

It was yet early in the evening, and hushed sounds were coming from the adjoining stalls. Many of the animals had not bedded down and were chewing the straw and grain they had been given. Others, with newborns too, were suckling their little ones. Still others had curled down to rest, even sleeping. A smile tugged at Alon's lips; he loved animals of all kinds.

A few of the animals had slipped their confines and wandered to the lighted stall where the man and woman were tending their child. No one seemed to mind that the animals were curious too.

Peering over the man's shoulder, an old grey donkey appeared interested in the baby. It stood there, quietly chewing a mouthful of hay. Then, surprising Alon, a young goat and a very new lamb wandered into the enclosure. Kicking and playing, the lamb ran up to the manger where the baby lay. Seeing the child there, it jumped back, tripping and falling on its side. "Beehhh," the lamb called out, and then jumped up and ran away, causing the man and woman to exchange a glance and a smile.

Unnoticed, Alon crouched down toward the back and to the side of the manger, just outside old stall boards. Kneeling, he was still and watched the young family for a few moments. Then, needing to rid himself of his bag and the shepherd's crook, he laid them down beside him.

Alon could see the baby's face and was watching as it opened its eyes. With only a small distance separating them, it was as though this tiny child was looking at him. He smiled to himself, and as he watched, Alon imagined that the tiny infant smiled too. There was something special about this child's face, especially the eyes.

Others had now gathered around the enclosure. There were merchants from the village, a few travelers from the road, some other shepherds, and the curious who had also seen the star.

Alon heard a man behind him whisper, "It's the Messiah, you know. The one the prophets foretold." He added, "The Angels told the mother she would give birth to a son." Elbowing the man beside him, the speaker nodded toward the manger. "He is here to lead us from our bondage … from the Romans."

Alon glanced toward the men, then back at the child. The boy thought, *But, he's just a little baby.*

He recalled the Roman soldiers he had seen and tried to avoid in the last two days. Alon had seen no slaves with them. Remembering though, there had been a time in the last year when their herd passed near a site where a large building was being erected. Alon's father had pointed to a line of men passing stones one to another.

"Those men are slaves," his father had told him. "They have no choice about what they are doing. The Romans have the power of life and death over them." As they watched, the leather thongs of a whip lashed out from an overseer, leaving angry red marks across the back of a slave. "That," Alon's father told him, "is the plight of the Jewish people." Alon and his father had seen similar acts on other occasions.

As the shepherd boy considered what the man behind him had said about the baby being the one to save them, there was a disturbance out on the road. Heads turned. Though darkness was upon the village, the sounds of hooves made Alon realize someone new was approaching the stable. *More than one,* he thought, a shiver coursing through his body. *Could it be the Romans?* He glanced back at the baby.

Others, appearing ill at ease, looked out to the street. Everyone feared the Romans. Alon's glance followed the others. Perhaps, the soldiers had come to arrest the gathering of mostly Jews. The boy secured his belongings and placed a hand on the board separating him from the stall. He was ready to run.

Then those who had gathered in front of the stall parted to let the new arrivals enter. And they didn't just part. Surprised, Alon watched as heads and bodies tilted forward, bowing. Whoever was coming must be important.

The boy glanced down at himself. Alon was suddenly aware of the dusty and tattered shepherd's garb he wore and how poor he must look. He was virtually in rags. Alon unconsciously attempted to make himself smaller in the space he occupied at the corner of the stall.

Still watching as the crowd parted, Alon could see out to the road and watched in fascination. Several men rode into the light of the stable, three on camels and the last on a horse. The boy's eyes were drawn to this animal. It was black and the largest stallion Alon had ever seen. Not even the Romans rode horses like this.

All the animals were magnificent. They were obviously well fed and cared for. On their backs were beautiful blankets under saddles of the finest leather with inlays along the edges that glistened in the light. Alon wondered if the decorations were of silver.

The mounted riders were magnificent too.

"Kings," Alon heard someone say.

"No ... Magi," another whispered. "... Wise men."

Those gathered stared in awe. They couldn't believe what they were seeing.

With everyone looking their way, the riders dismounted, those on camels calling for the animals to kneel so each man could expertly slide to the ground. The man on the horse swung himself out of the saddle in one swift motion. Then they each busied themselves gathering boxes and other articles from bags attached to their saddles. The men were dressed in the finest robes of beautiful colors, belts with silver buckles, and high boots of polished leather.

When they had what they wanted from their mounts, the men turned and walked into the stable and toward the young family there with the newborn child. Then, surprising Alon and causing a stir among the entire gathering, the Magi kneeled at a reverent distance from the manger where the tiny boy-child was cradled.

These men who by their very presence commanded such respect, not only kneeled, but then prostrated themselves to the child in the manger. Alon, who knew so little outside of being a shepherd, recognized he was viewing something extraordinary.

Around him, Alon saw that others also knew they were witness to the coming of a very special child.

Maybe he is the Messiah, thought Alon.

Heads bowed, prayers could be heard in soft tones throughout the gathering.

And in each heart, the Angel's sang: Thanks be to God, for on this day, in the City of David, is born a savior …

Alon watched as the Magi then rose to their feet. Glancing about, the boy could see everyone watching the men closely. Holding the treasures they brought with them, the men moved closer to the manger and placed their wonderful gifts on the straw near the child. The young father and mother acknowledged the offerings with smiles and words of thanks on behalf of the little one.

Outside the boards separating him from the manger, Alon watched as a strong feeling came over him, an overwhelming desire to honor this child. *But I have nothing to give,* he thought. Alon had not even known where he was going when he left his family. He had only known that he must follow the star.

Now he was here in this special place. If he could believe his own feelings and all he was seeing around him, then he, Alon, was now in the presence of the Messiah.

Then he thought of the shepherd's crook. He looked down at it and remembered how it had come to be, how his grandfather had made it with his own hands. How it was expected the staff would one day be passed to another shepherd.

Alon looked at the baby. *If this tiny one really is the Messiah, then he has come to deliver the people from their Roman bondage. He has come to be their leader. Their shepherd?*

Resting there on his knees, his father's words came to the boy. "Your heart will tell you when it is time to pass this staff on to another shepherd." In this moment, Alon knew what he must do.

He reached down and touched the shepherd's crook, silently moving it beneath the boards and toward the manger. It was the only thing he had to give, and it was the right thing.

In the shadow of activity both in the stable and outside, Alon thought he could slip the shepherd's crook near the Magi's gifts without anyone noticing. He had almost succeeded when he realized someone was standing beside him outside the stall. Before he even glanced up to the man, Alon could see polished boots and a flowing robe.

The individual who had ridden the black stallion stood looking down at Alon. His stern expression burned into the boy's eyes and mind. This man must think him a trespasser, an impostor trying to place his insignificant gift with those of the Magi. Alon wanted to run away.

But then the man kneeled down at Alon's side and smiled. It was as if the sun had come from behind clouds on a cold windy day.

"Is this your gift for the child?" Alon was asked.

Hesitating, he nodded timidly.

"Is this all you have?"

Again, he nodded, but this time Alon was ashamed.

This is ... all I have.

The man saw through Alon's eyes to his heart. He spoke gently.

"Do not be ashamed," he said. "These Kings and I have given only a part of what we own. You," he said pointing toward the shepherd's crook, "have given all that you possess." He paused for a moment. "In God's sight, your gift is greater than any of ours." Then, reaching through the boards, the man picked up Alon's staff and placed it gently and reverently across the top of the Magi's gifts.

Only then did Alon look up at the others gathered near the manger. Everyone was smiling at him, even the Magi.

Touching Alon's shoulder, the man spoke again. "When you return to your home, know that the Christ Child will have need of your gift and will treasure it."

The next morning, Alon began the journey back to his father's herd. By midmorning, his feet were dusty and sore, and he was hungry. Other travelers had given him a few scraps to eat, but it was not enough. Alon longed to be back with his father and uncles where he would be fed and could rest. He couldn't wait to tell them about the baby and the Magi.

Topping a short hill, the boy had already walked for several hours when he heard hooves clattering along in the dust behind him. He moved to the side of the road and stood still, fearing the rider to be a Roman soldier. The horse drew short and stopped beside Alon.

"Have you far to go?" the rider asked. The voice was familiar.

Turning and shading his eyes with a hand, Alon looked up. It was the man who had spoken to him at the stable. The black stallion pranced about and snorted.

"Another day and night until I reach my father's herd," the boy said in answer to the rider's question.

"Then join me. I am going your way."

Alon hesitated. Could he be so bold as to take the magnificent stranger's offer?

The man did not wait. "Come," he said.

Reaching down, he took Alon's hand, easily swinging him up behind the saddle. With the boy's hand on the stranger's hip, they rode on.

There was food in a saddle bag, and the man shared it with Alon. He asked about Alon's family and life as a shepherd. The man listened to the boy's words. Finally, he told Alon he had a young son also, and two daughters. He sounded proud of them.

On horseback, the distance passed quickly. By late afternoon, they had reached the valley where Alon's father and uncles were grazing the herds. Alon pointed them out to his new friend.

When they arrived, Alon's father was surprised to see his son riding with this rich man.

"This is my father," Alon said to the man.

While exchanging greetings, the father realized Alon was not carrying the shepherd's crook he had been given. He asked about it.

"If the Christ Child is going to lead our people," Alon told his father, "he will need a staff, for he will surely be our shepherd."

The father listened.

"When I was near the baby, I believed he really is the Messiah," Alon told his father. He paused, glancing at the man there with them. "... I still believe that."

The stranger had remained silent, allowing Alon to answer his father's questions. Now the man asked if he could speak. Alon's father nodded while pulling nervously at his beard.

"As I told your son in Bethlehem, I believe his gift is worthier in God's eyes than all those given by the Magi." His hand reached out and tousled the boy's hair. "Your son gave everything. We did not."

The pleased expression on the father's face revealed his feelings when he looked at his son. With a hand on Alon's shoulder, he said, "I am proud of you."

"I must continue my journey," Alon's friend said after a few moments. "My family will be waiting."

They said goodbye, and the man swung up on his mount. Alon and his father watched as the big black horse and its rider galloped away.

Standing there on the hill, Alon's father spoke to him. "You are a good son."

~ *To the Cross* ~

THIRTY-THREE YEARS HAD PASSED SINCE Alon followed a star to the manger in Bethlehem. Now a much older shepherd, he stands alone at the top of a rock-strewn hill. Deep in thought while keeping an eye on his herd, Alon is gazing down into a valley west of Jerusalem. As a boy, he had herded sheep here with his father. As wandering shepherds do, he had returned to these hills and valleys many times over the years. Now, with a stooped and ailing back and using a fig tree limb as a cane, he doubted that he would come this way again.

Leaning on the cane and with his hand on a rock, he thought of the shepherd's crook he had left for the Christ Child. The old man smiled, realizing he had never questioned that decision. Not once in all the years since that night. Alon thought of his father and smiled again. His father had been proud of him for giving the staff to the Christ Child.

Life had changed in many ways since Alon tracked the star. Following his return from Bethlehem at thirteen, the boy had worked with his family's herd in the nomadic tradition. In his early twenties, he lost his father who had been his friend and teacher. Remembering, Alon was happy his father had lived to know he had a grandson.

As a young man not yet twenty, Alon had taken a wife, and she had given him a son. Alon brought up the child as he had been raised, and life had been taken up by those duties. He had spent the ensuing years protecting the sheep and moving them to new grazing in the hills near Jerusalem. For the old shepherd, each day and night had been much like those that came before it. He expected no change as he neared the end of his years. Leaning on the cane, he thought of other times—both good and bad.

Some memories though, he tried to avoid entirely. His own son had been taken as a slave when the boy was barely becoming a man. The Romans had stolen the son away as he and a friend were walking along the main road, returning from a local market. If another shepherd had not witnessed the taking of the two young men, Alon would never have known what happened to his boy.

To no avail, the shepherd had tried to locate his son, to find out where he had been taken. The boy and his friend had vanished without a trace, never to be heard from again. Alon was not without guilt, wondering often if he could have instructed his son in better ways to avoid the Romans. Could Alon have saved his son?

The old shepherd sighed, a hand near his heart. *Some memories and thoughts are better forgotten.*

Life had not been easy. Through the years, the Romans had held a firm hand on Israel, requiring much in the way of taxes and obedience. Expectations were often dashed, and dreams were better kept inside one's mind. Only whispers of a redeemer being at hand allowed hope to remain within reach. Almost ...

One day in the spring, the old shepherd was talking with a friend whose herd grazed on the hills near his own. The shepherd asked if Alon had heard talk of a man who was traveling about the land and speaking to the people. It was said this man was teaching a special message, one of love and forgiveness. It was even rumored the man had performed miracles. Some went so far as to say this teacher had come to lead the Jews from their bondage.

Who is this person? Alon wondered. *Where had he come from?*

The friend was excited about the teacher. "It is said he was born in Bethlehem under a mysterious star."

Upon hearing this, Alon felt the hair rise on his neck. A shudder ran through his body as his eyes were drawn to the east. Steadying himself on the fig tree cane, Alon thought of the child he had journeyed to see and the gift he had left behind. Alon could almost feel the shepherd's crook in his hands in those moments before he had placed it on the straw near the manger.

"How old is this man?" Alon asked. *Could that tiny baby have grown into the man who is now teaching the people to care for all men and to forgive their transgressors? Could he really be the one who would free the people of Israel from the Romans?*

"I do not know his age," the friend responded, "but he must be a man of some years, otherwise the people would not listen to him."

Alon was lost in his thoughts for a time before he realized his friend was again speaking to him.

"Some who have been with this teacher whisper he is the Messiah," the friend said softly.

Alon, shocked at this statement, looked at the man and said, "Surely you misunderstood."

"No. That is what they are saying. You must go and hear him too." The friend paused. "Then you will know."

"But how can I do that?" Alon asked, his eyes on the sheep. "I must tend to my herd."

But the old shepherd thought about it. The boy in him remembered the journey many years ago when he followed a star and found an infant in a manger. The people there had called that child the Messiah. They said he would lead them from their bondage and troubles.

The Magi had been there too. They had traveled great distances and brought gifts to the child in the manger. With their deeds and their words, they proclaimed the child to be their King … Their Messiah?

And Alon remembered again, he had given his shepherd's crook to the baby in the manger. It was the only thing he had to give. He also remembered the words spoken to him on that night so long ago. "You have given all that you possess. In God's sight, your gift is greater than any of ours."

The friend interrupted Alon's thoughts again. "He is coming this way tomorrow. I am going to hear him speak. Will you come with me?"

"Yes," Alon whispered without having to think about it.

Leaving others to watch the sheep, the two men left at sunrise and walked until mid-afternoon. The old shepherd's ever-present cane steadied his slowing steps.

A crowd had gathered on a hill just off the road. According to several, the teacher and those who traveled with him had been seen in this area. It was said this person would come and talk to those gathered at this place.

Alon's friend moved through the throng finding out what he could. The crowd had settled near a slow-moving stream. Those nearby talked quietly amongst themselves as they waited.

"Could he really be the Messiah?" Alon heard someone say. Listening, he heard another proclaim that the teacher was the Christ—the Redeemer, as some called him. Others simply called him Jesus. Everyone spoke of him with reverence and looked forward to the evening when the teacher would speak to them.

Alon's friend returned, saying, "He will be here soon." They found a spot near the rocks where the teacher would stand and seated themselves to wait. Placing the fig tree limb at his side, the old shepherd rubbed a knee and was grateful for the respite.

There was activity near the stream a short time later, and a man followed by several others climbed atop the rocks. At once, chatter ceased on the hillside, all eyes focused on the teacher. Many stood, bowing toward him, their arms raised in reverence.

The man stepped forward and held up his hands. The gesture once more stilled the crowd, causing them to sit quietly and give him their attention. He wore a white outer garment, and Alon could see sandals on the man's dusty feet beneath the robe.

Jesus began to speak. His voice was soft, but it carried to all who were gathered. Gazing about, Alon had the feeling each could hear as though Jesus was standing near them.

Every pair of eyes were on the man from Galilee.

Alon refocused his own attention on this man who was standing only a few feet away. He listened carefully, wanting to understand what others found in the words of this ordinary-appearing individual.

He was younger than Alon, but otherwise, the man didn't look special. He was no taller nor better robed than others standing with him on the rock shelf. He didn't appear to be exceptional.

But, Alon realized, there *was* something different about him.

When the teacher looked in his direction, the man's eyes appeared to search Alon out. Often, as he spoke, Jesus seemed to look toward the old shepherd. For some reason, this attention bothered Alon.

Finding himself more uncomfortable as the minutes passed, Alon shifted about nervously. Try as he might though, the old shepherd couldn't escape the feeling that Jesus was speaking directly to him. Alon glanced about, wondering if everyone had that sensation—that Jesus was talking only to them.

The man spoke of forgiveness. "For if you forgive men when they sin against you, your heavenly Father will also forgive you."

The old and disturbing thought in his own life was immediately upon Alon. *The Roman soldiers took my son. I despise them— surely, I hate them.*

Those eyes found Alon again as the teacher continued. "And when you stand praying, if you hold anything against anyone, forgive him, so that your Father in heaven may forgive you your sins."

Alon looked away. The old shepherd was hearing commands he was not prepared to obey. How could he forgive the men who took his son?

As the teacher continued, Alon gradually began to relax and listen closer to his words. The subject had changed, but the lesson was basic. "Be kind to your fellow man. Treat him as you would want to be treated. And that applies," Jesus said, "to everyone from your own family to your neighbor and to the stranger you may meet along a dusty road."

Alon listened. The words made sense.

All too soon, it was over. Jesus finished and then stepped down off the rocks, speaking with those who gathered around him.

Curious, Alon edged closer. He leaned in to listen as Jesus spoke with a group of shepherds. Without warning, Jesus reached out with his eyes and garnered Alon's attention as he had earlier. Unable to look away, Alon felt himself drawn to this stranger.

He listened, exchanging glances. Then the teacher moved on to others.

Alon tried but couldn't get close to Jesus again that afternoon. Finally, he left to find his friend, the teacher's words about forgiveness on his mind.

Deciding to wait until morning to return to their herds, the old shepherd and his friend found a place to lay out their bedrolls. His friend then went to finish a conversation with someone he had met earlier in the afternoon.

As evening fell, Alon, alone and uneasy, walked the surrounding hills gathering his thoughts. His life had been spent in a solitary manner, shepherding the family's herd. Thinking back, he didn't believe the years would be much different even if the Romans did not control Israel. He would still have lived the life of a shepherd, walking these hills and guarding his sheep.

The exception in his life was the loss of his son. Five years had gone by. There had not been a day when Alon didn't think of the boy. If the Romans hadn't taken him, his son would have married by now and be raising sons of his own.

Forgive them? Alon didn't think it was possible.

As he walked along kicking at a loose stone here and there and thinking of the day's events, Alon became aware of someone else on the hill near him. Assuming one of the other shepherds had been restless too, Alon raised a hand in greeting. He recognized the voice of the man who spoke back to him.

This was not one of the shepherds.

Jesus was sitting on a rock overlooking the valley and down to the stream where he had talked with the gathered crowd in the late afternoon. He smiled and spoke to Alon with that gentle voice.

With a gesture, he said, "Come. Sit with me."

Alon felt drawn to do as he was asked. He climbed up and sat near Jesus. When he was settled, the teacher smiled, touching Alon's shoulder with gentle fingers, saying, "I hoped you would come this way. I wanted to speak with you."

They talked for a while. Jesus asked about Alon's family, and then he wondered aloud about life in these hills tending the sheep. The old shepherd found it easy to talk to this man. He had a calm manner about him, and they spoke of many things. Alon described his life as a nomad and a shepherd. Jesus, in turn, spoke of his own journey and his teachings.

"I am a shepherd too," Jesus said. "I have come to provide a way for the people to be safe and protected." He paused, then finished his thought. "The time of my teaching is almost over. I must return to my father's house."

Listening, Alon did not understand what the teacher was telling him. He wondered where this house was located, where this teacher's journey would take him?

Finally, Alon asked who would lead when Jesus returned to his father. The teacher told him to listen to the disciples. "They will show you the way to my father's house."

Then Jesus looked at Alon and said, "I know there is hate in you for those who took your son." He paused and then added, "They will never know if you forgive them, but you will know … and my Father will know."

The teacher and the old shepherd looked at each other, their eyes locked in silent understanding. Alon, in that moment, knew the decision granting forgiveness was his alone to make. He realized, too, that no one could change events already past—not him, not the Roman soldiers, not even Jesus. The only thing that could be changed was how he chose to deal with the loss of his son. That choice, too, was his alone.

I will think on it. Forgiveness has not been in my thoughts ... until now. Alon glanced at the teacher, receiving only a smile. *Yes, it is my decision.*

As the sun set on the western horizon, Jesus said it was time for him to go. He slipped himself off the rock and picked up his staff. Alon started to say goodbye. Having taken a step down the hill, Jesus turned, and for the first time, Alon noticed the shepherd's crook he carried.

Jesus followed his eyes, glancing at it too. He then handed the staff to Alon.

"You are a shepherd. Take this," he said. "A young shepherd boy gave it to me many years ago." Jesus smiled, a knowing look in his eye. "It has helped me along many a rocky path." Then he added, "I will have no need of it in the days I have left."

For the first time, Alon looked closely at the staff. Even after all the passing years, the old shepherd immediately recognized it. It had been his father's staff ... the one his father had given Alon on the night he set out to follow the star. Alon had given it to the Christ Child.

As the old shepherd stared at the staff, Jesus spoke to him. Pausing and holding Alon's eyes once more, the teacher said, "Thank you for making my steps here less difficult."

With those words, Jesus turned and walked away.

Alon watched until the teacher was out of sight. Finally, the old shepherd placed his fig tree limb on a nearby rock, his fingers lingering on it for a moment. It had served him well. Perhaps another wandering shepherd with slowing steps could use the cane.

In Alon's hand, the shepherd's crook now felt at home. His father would have been pleased for it to be back with the family. He would have been happy, too, to have known of its journey.

Alon looked forward to morning when he could start back toward his own herd. Then, for the first time, he realized he no longer felt the malice in his heart for the Romans who took his son. Perhaps, he *could* forgive them.

Maybe someday, like Jesus, *his* son would come home too. Alon would gladly give the shepherd's staff to him. And Alon would tell his son the story.

www.ingramcontent.com/pod-product-compliance
Lightning Source LLC
Chambersburg PA
CBHW072305130726
47910CB00012B/2533

9 780989 720182